SEVEN MILES TO FREEDOM

THE ROBERT SMALLS STORY

by JANET HALFMANN
illustrated by DUANE SMITH

Lee & Low Books Inc.
New York

Robert Smalls's dreams of freedom began in his hometown of Beaufort, South Carolina, the largest town on a cluster of plantation islands down the coast from Charleston. He was born there in 1839 in the slave quarters on the McKee family's property.

Robert's mother was a house servant, and when he was about six years old Robert also began working in the McKee household. He brushed Master McKee's horse, carried his hunting bow, and baited his fishing hook. Good-spirited and talkative, Robert was the master's favorite.

As a favored house servant, Robert had an easier life than most slaves. Even so, from the time he was a young boy, he witnessed the evils of slavery. At neighboring plantations he saw slaves whipped until they were bloody, punished for the simplest things—getting to the fields a few moments late, missing a patch of weeds, not working fast enough. In town Robert watched boys and girls his own age sold like animals on the auction block.

Although the McKees were kind to him, Robert grew to hate slavery. More and more he wished to be free.

In 1851, when Robert was twelve, the McKees sent him to live and work in Charleston. All day and into the night he waited tables and made deliveries to rooms at the elegant Planter's Hotel. Robert earned five dollars a month but had to give the money to his master.

Anytime Robert wasn't working he headed to the waterfront. He watched the boats of all shapes and sizes, fascinated by how they could sail anywhere in the world.

Robert liked talking to the workers on the ships. In hushed voices they told him stories about "Up North," where all colored people were free to learn to read and write. Free to keep the money they earned. Free to make their own decisions. Robert's eyes lit up with hope. Someday he would have those freedoms too.

Eager to spend more time at the waterfront, Robert got permission from Master McKee to work at the docks loading and unloading cargo from ships. Robert worked hard. He was smart and dependable, and by age fifteen he was foreman of a crew, directing men twice his age.

Eventually Robert grew to dislike the routine of the job, so he began working in the shipyard, making and rigging sails. Robert enjoyed testing the sails on boats in the water, and he learned to navigate narrow channels, gliding carefully past hidden rocks. His boss boasted that Robert had the makings of a wheelman, the title given to colored boat pilots in the South.

When Robert was seventeen he met Hannah Jones, a Charleston hotel maid who was the slave of Samuel Kingman. Robert loved Hannah's sparkling eyes and sharp intelligence, and wanted to spend his life with her. In order to marry and live together, the couple worked out agreements with their masters. Robert and Hannah would find their own jobs. Every month Robert would give McKee fifteen dollars, and Hannah would give Kingman seven dollars. Any other money the couple earned would be their own.

Robert and Hannah married on December 24, 1856, and in February 1858, their first child, Elizabeth, was born. As Robert held the tiny bundle, he was saddened by the realization that Elizabeth did not belong to them. She was the property of Hannah's master. So Robert made a deal to buy his wife's and daughter's freedom for eight hundred dollars. Although Robert was still enslaved, the arrangement would allow Hannah and Elizabeth to go wherever he went.

Robert and Hannah didn't know how they would save that much money, but they were going to try.

In the evenings, by candlelight, Hannah sewed garments for the wealthy women of Charleston while Robert studied charts and maps of the harbor, rivers, creeks, and channels. He noted the location of every reef, sandbar, and current.

Soon Robert was expertly navigating the waterways, delivering boats to plantations all along the coast. During summers, he worked as a sailor on a coastal schooner. His dedication and skill earned him a reputation as one of the best boat handlers in Charleston.

After three years Robert and Hannah had saved seven hundred dollars. The couple were close to their goal, but a storm was brewing in the nation.

By the spring of 1861, Charleston was at the eye of the storm. For a long time, northern and southern states had been arguing about slavery. As the country expanded west, southerners wanted slavery allowed in the new territories. Northerners did not. In 1860 Abraham Lincoln, who opposed the spread of slavery, was elected president. South Carolina responded by breaking away from the United States. Several other southern states followed. Together, they formed the Confederate States of America. The northern states remained the United States of America, or the Union.

The Confederacy quickly took charge of many military forts in the South, but the Union kept control of Fort Sumter in Charleston Harbor. On April 12, 1861, a battle for Fort Sumter ended in the fort's surrender to the Confederacy. A civil war between the North and South had begun.

For slaves such as Robert and Hannah war brought uncertainty, but also hope. If the North won, slavery would end.

Commercial boat traffic in and out of
Charleston Harbor slowed to a trickle. Soon
there was no work for Robert in the shipyard.
In July he took a job as a deckhand on the
Planter, a 147-foot, wood-burning steamer.
The boat once hauled cotton but had been
converted into an armed Confederate ship for
carrying soldiers, equipment, and supplies.

All that summer on the *Planter* Robert
helped build up Confederate defenses in the
harbor and along the coast. He laid mines,
destroyed a lighthouse, and built new forts.
But in his heart Robert wanted the Union to
win the war.

Robert's navigational skills and knowledge
of the waterways impressed the *Planter*'s
officers. He was promoted to wheelman, a
position of trust and honor. Now responsible
for steering the boat, Robert learned the secret
steam whistle signals for passing the harbor's
many forts.

In late 1861 freedom suddenly grew closer for Robert and Hannah. The Union navy captured Port Royal, just down the coast from Charleston. A Union fleet set up a blockade at the entrance to Charleston Harbor. Looking through the captain's field glasses, Robert could see the northern ships. The Union lines and freedom were within reach—only seven miles away.

This gave Robert renewed hope and determination, as did the birth of his son, Robert Jr. Now more than ever, Robert knew he had to find a way to freedom, for himself and his growing family.

When the opportunity finally came, it started with a joke. One evening the boat's white officers went ashore to spend the night, even though this was against military rules. Jokingly, one of the crew plopped the captain's straw hat on Robert's head. Robert crossed his arms and strutted about just like the short, strongly built captain. Everyone laughed. Given Robert's similar build, the resemblance was amazing.

Suddenly Robert became serious and told the men to keep the joke to themselves. He had an idea.

Robert shared his plan with Hannah. On a night when the officers were ashore, he and the crew would steal the *Planter*. Their families would hide at a nearby wharf and be picked up on the way. Wearing the captain's hat and responding with the secret steam whistle signals, Robert would trick the fort guards into letting the ship pass. He would sail the *Planter* out to the Union fleet and to freedom.

Hannah asked him what would happen if they were caught. Robert told her they would probably be shot. Hannah was quiet for a moment, and then agreed to go along. She too was willing to risk her life and the lives of their children for a chance at freedom.

Robert explained the plan to his crewmates and made them promise to keep it secret. He also told them that if something went wrong, they would sink the ship rather than allow themselves to be captured. If it didn't go down fast enough, they would all clasp hands and jump overboard. The men agreed. They trusted Robert, and they too yearned for freedom.

The timing was left to Robert. He had to choose the right moment.

Day after day Robert watched and listened. In the spring of 1862, an opportunity arose. The *Planter*'s crew was to move four cannons guarding a river southwest of Charleston to a fort being built in the harbor. The captain wanted the move completed by dark on Monday, May 12. The officers planned to go ashore that night and stay until morning.

Robert realized this was the chance he had been waiting for.

On May 12 the *Planter* traveled to the river to transfer the cannons. Robert and his crewmates knew how valuable these weapons would be to the Union. They planned to delay the delivery of the cannons and escape with them.

The men purposely worked slowly. They fumbled knots and dropped lines. By the time all four cannons were on board it was late afternoon. Robert's plan was working. Delivery to the fort would have to wait until morning.

Robert's mind raced as he guided the *Planter* back to its dock in the harbor. The time for the escape was nearing. Throbbing with anticipation, he was careful not to let his excitement show.

Finally the officers went ashore, trusting Robert to have the boat ready for an early start in the morning.

Robert immediately gathered the crew and went over the plan once more. Then the men sprang into action, loading stacks of firewood on deck to power the steam boilers and double-checking every instrument. Robert put on a white ruffled shirt, a dress jacket, and the captain's wide-brimmed straw hat.

It was three o'clock in the morning by the time a full head of steam hissed in the boilers. The Confederate and South Carolina flags were raised to the top of the mast. In the pilothouse Robert gripped the wheel as he backed the *Planter* away from its dock. The ship coasted upstream a short way and stopped. A rowboat stole from the *Planter* to fetch the families of the crew from a boat they had hidden in since nightfall.

Robert peered uneasily at the dark water, waiting for the rowboat to return with its precious load. After a few long minutes, it appeared. In pin-drop quiet the families boarded and were led below deck.

With everyone safely aboard, Robert started down the harbor. He blew the whistle to leave the dockside, and it was answered. Fighting a strong urge to rush, Robert eased the ship cautiously into the open water. He had to stay calm. His family and the others on board were all counting on him. Robert's patience paid off. The shore guard saw the *Planter* leave but did not stop it.

The *Planter*'s paddle wheels cut through the dark water with a steady churn. Castle Pinckney and Fort Ripley were passed easily. Fort Johnson loomed ahead, its walls bristling with cannons. His palms sweaty, Robert reached for the cord of the steam whistle. He blew the secret signal and prayed. The lookout signaled back: *All right*. Robert breathed a sigh of relief.

As the ship neared the massive walls of Fort Sumter, Robert saw that dawn was breaking. The *Planter* had lost time bucking the incoming tide. In the early-morning light the lookout might be able to tell that Robert was not the captain. An anxious crewmate told Robert to make a dash for freedom. But Robert knew that if the *Planter* sped by the fort, cannons would be fired on them, smashing the ship to pieces. He continued at the slow, even speed the guards expected.

Robert asked a crewmate to take the wheel. He pulled down the captain's straw hat to shadow his face and stood at the window of the pilothouse. Under his dress jacket Robert's heart thumped loudly. Mimicking the captain, he folded his arms across his chest. Then, slowly, Robert sounded the signal.

WOOOOO, WOOOOO, WOO!

From the pilothouse to the engine room to the hold, bodies tensed. The response was taking too long. . . . Finally, the *Planter* received the signal to pass. Robert mopped sweat from his brow. There were only a few more miles to go and one more fort to pass.

Fort Moultrie came up quickly, and the *Planter* passed without trouble. Robert kept the same deliberate pace until the ship was out of range of the last Confederate gun. Then he ordered FULL STEAM AHEAD! Clouds of black smoke belched from the smokestack. The boat surged forward, its paddle wheels whisking the water white.

A Confederate lookout saw the burst of speed through his field glasses. When the ship headed out to sea, he knew something was wrong. Frantically the lookout signaled an alert. Lights flashed and flickered, but it was too late. No Confederate guns could reach the *Planter* now.

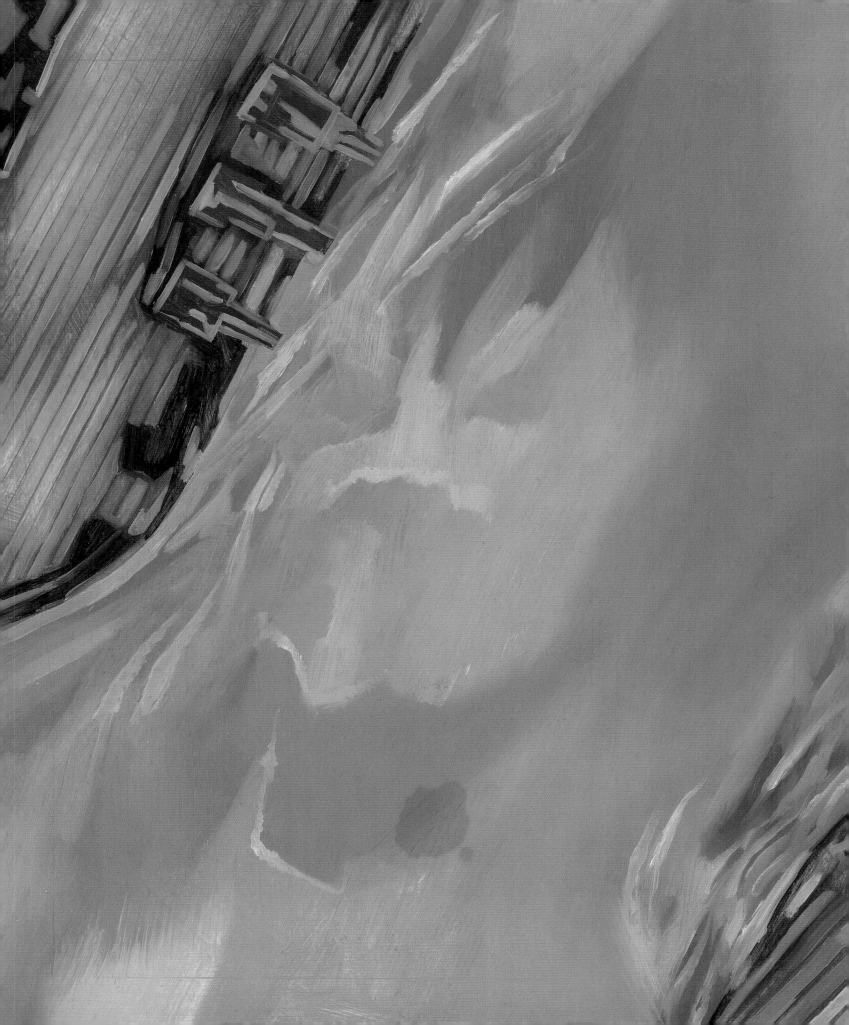

The Union ships and freedom waited just ahead, but the *Planter* still was not safe. From the beginning Robert had worried most about these final moments. Union sailors would be prepared to fire on any boat coming from Charleston. Robert had to convince them not to shoot. Ordering the flags lowered and Hannah's best white sheet raised as a sign of surrender, Robert sailed toward the *Onward*, the nearest ship of the Union fleet. In the early morning fog, the Union lookout couldn't see the white sheet. He saw only a big boat speeding through the haze and mist. He thought it was a Confederate ship coming to ram them.

The lookout shouted an alarm. The *Onward* turned, pointing a row of guns at the *Planter*. Leaning hard on the wheel, Robert swung the boat around. With the turn the white sheet caught the wind and flapped open in the ocean breeze. Suddenly a Union sailor cried out that he saw a white flag.

The *Onward*'s captain ordered the gunners to hold their fire and instructed the *Planter* to come alongside.

Men, women, and children ran out onto the deck of the *Planter*. Robert, standing straight and proud, stepped forward and raised the captain's hat high in the air. He shouted that he had brought the Union a load of Confederate cannons.

When the *Onward*'s surprised captain climbed aboard, Robert told him he thought the *Planter* might be of some service to "Uncle Abe" Lincoln. Then Robert turned the Confederate ship and its cannons over to the Union navy.

The white sheet was lowered. As the *Planter*'s crew and their families gazed up, the Union flag rose skyward. Robert and Hannah held their children close, their hearts full of hope. On this morning of a new day, they were on their way to freedom.

AFTERWORD

While the South fumed over the loss of the *Planter*, the North praised Robert Smalls as a national hero. *The New York Herald* declared his action "one of the most heroic and daring adventures since the war commenced." Robert was employed as a civilian pilot for the Union navy. He met with President Lincoln, and helped convince him to let African Americans enlist in the Union army. Robert also spoke to crowds in the North to gain aid for former slaves.

On December 1, 1863, Robert had another risky adventure aboard the *Planter*. He was piloting the ship for the Union when it came under intense fire in South Carolina. The captain of the *Planter* ordered Robert to surrender the boat, then hid in the coal bunker. Knowing the crew of former slaves could be killed if captured, Robert quickly took the wheel, steering the ship to outrun the Confederates. For his bravery Robert was named as the *Planter*'s new captain, making him the first African American captain of a United States vessel.

Throughout the war Robert piloted several Union ships, taking part in seventeen battles. During these years Hannah gave birth to the couple's second daughter, Sarah. Sadly, their son, Robert Jr., died of smallpox.

Robert and his family remained in Beaufort after the war. He purchased the McKee house, where he had once been a slave, and learned to read and write. In 1868, along with seventy-six African Americans and forty-eight whites, Robert helped write a new democratic state constitution. The document included his proposal for the creation of South Carolina's first free system of public schools for all children. Robert also won a seat in the state legislature, where he fought for equal rights for African Americans, and became active in the state militia, rising to the rank of major general.

Robert was elected to the United States Congress in 1875. During his five terms, he called for the elimination of race discrimination in the army, introduced a petition to give women the right to vote, and fought against the policy of separate railroad cars for African Americans.

When Robert's congressional career came to an end, he was appointed the collector of customs in Beaufort, holding the position for nearly twenty years. Hannah died in 1883. Robert later remarried and had another son.

In 1895 South Carolina revised its state constitution, legally restricting the right of African Americans to vote—a right that was granted by an amendment to the United States Constitution in 1870. As one of only six African American delegates at the 1895 convention, Robert argued eloquently to preserve his people's right to vote. Still, this right was all but taken away by the limitations placed on it. Robert and other African American delegates refused to sign the document to adopt these changes. With African American rights slipping away, Robert continued to fight unfair laws, giving speeches and reaching out to members of the United States Congress for support.

In his later years Robert often visited with African American students in Beaufort. He told them about the accomplishments of their people and stressed the importance of education. Robert died in 1915 at the age of seventy-five. His funeral was the largest ever held in Beaufort.

The United States Army christened the *Major General Robert Smalls* in 2004. This ship is the first army vessel ever named after an African American.

> "My race needs no special defense, for the past history of them in this country proves them to be the equal of any people. All they need is an equal chance in the battle of life."

—Robert Smalls's words from the 1895 constitutional convention, which also appear on a statue near his grave in Beaufort

AUTHOR'S SOURCES

A.M.E. Review, "Capt. Robert Smalls Addresses the General Conference of 1864," no. 70 (January-March, 1955): 22-23, 31.

Blassingame, John W., Ed. "Robert Smalls," *Slave Testimony: Two Centuries of Letters, Speeches, Interviews, and Autobiographies*. Baton Rouge, LA: Louisiana State University Press, 1977.

Charleston Daily Courier, "The Steamer Planter," May 14, 1862.

Cowley, Charles. *The Romance of History in* The Black County, *and the Romance of War in the Career of Gen. Robert Smalls, The Hero of the Planter*. Lowell, MA: 1882.

Du Pont, Samuel Francis. *Samuel Francis Du Pont: A Selection from His Civil War Letters*, ed. John D. Hayes, Vol. 2. Ithaca, NY: Cornell University Press, 1969.

Guthrie, James M. "Camp-Fires of the Afro-American, 1889." In *The Negro's Civil War: How American Negroes Felt and Acted During the War for the Union* by James M. McPherson. New York: Ballantine Books, 1991.

Letters of William Robert Smalls to Dorothy Sterling 1955-1956, Amistad Research Center, Tulane University, New Orleans.

Miller, Edward A., Jr., *Gullah Statesman*. Columbia, SC: University of South Carolina Press, 1995.

New York Daily Tribune, "Robert Smalls, the Negro Pilot," September 10, 1862.

New York Herald, "Heroism of Nine Colored Men," May 18, 1862.

"Robert Smalls: Official Website and Information Center," The Robert Smalls Foundation, www.robertsmalls.org.

Sterling, Dorothy. *Captain of the Planter*. New York: Pocket Books, 1968.

U.S. House of Representatives. Committee on Naval Affairs. *Authorizing the President to Place Robert Smalls on the Retired List of the Navy*, 47th Cong., 2d sess., Jan. 23, 1883. Rep. 1887. In *Men of Mark* by William J. Simmons. Cleveland, OH: Geo. M. Rewell & Co., 1887.

U.S. Naval War Records Office. *Official Records of the Union and Confederate Navies in the War of the Rebellion*. Washington, DC: Govt. Printing Office, 1894-1922, series 1, vol. 12: 820-826. Series 2, vol. 1: 180.

U.S. War Dept., *The War of the Rebellion: a Compilation of the Official Records of the Union and Confederate Armies*, Washington, DC: Govt. Printing Office, 1880-1901, series 1, vol. 14: 13-15, 502-503, 506, 509.

Uya, Okon Edet. *From Slavery to Public Service: Robert Smalls 1839-1915*. New York: Oxford University Press, 1971.

Washington, J. Irwin, Sr. "General Robert Smalls," *Colored American Magazine*, vol. 7 (June 1904): 424-31.

In memory of the thousands of African Americans
who helped win the Civil War.—J.H.

•••••

To the men and women in the armed forces who are
serving abroad in the Middle East, for your bravery.

To my family and friends for support.

I thank the Lord for blessing the works of my hands.—D.S.

ACKNOWLEDGMENTS

I especially wish to thank Kitt Alexander, founder of the Robert Smalls Legacy Foundation, for help with research sources and for reading the manuscript. I also wish to thank Richard W. Hatcher III, Historian, Fort Sumter National Monument, for answering questions. Thanks to the Amistad Research Center, Beaufort County Library, Robert Smalls Middle School, Wilberforce University Archives and Special Collections, New York Public Library, University of Wisconsin-Milwaukee Libraries, and Milwaukee County Federated Library System, for providing reference materials. A special thanks to my editors Momo Sanya and Jennifer Fox for helping me bring Robert Smalls's story to life.—J.H.

Manufactured in China

Book design by Susan and David Neuhaus/NeuStudio
Book production by The Kids at Our House

The text is set in 14-point Historical-Fell Type
The illustrations are rendered in oil on paper

10 9 8 7 6 5 4 3 2 1
First Edition

Library of Congress Cataloging-in-Publication Data
Halfmann, Janet.
Seven miles to freedom : the Robert Smalls story / by Janet Halfmann ; illustrated by Duane Smith. — 1st ed.
p. cm.
Summary: "A biography of Robert Smalls who, during the Civil War, commandeered the Confederate ship Planter to carry his family and twelve other slaves to freedom, and went on to become a United States Congressman working toward African American advancement"—Provided by publisher.
ISBN 978-1-60060-232-0
1. Smalls, Robert, 1839-1915—Juvenile literature. 2. African Americans—Biography—Juvenile literature. 3. Ship captains—United States—Biography—Juvenile literature. 4. Planter (Steamship)—Juvenile literature. 5. United States—History—Civil War, 1861-1865—Participation, African American—Juvenile literature. 6. African American legislators—Biography—Juvenile literature. 7. United States. Congress. House—Biography—Juvenile literature. 8. Fugitive slaves—South Carolina—Beaufort—Biography—Juvenile literature. 9. Beaufort (S.C.)—Biography—Juvenile literature. I. Smith, Duane, ill. II. Title.
E185.97.S6H34 2008
973.7'415092—dc22
2007029274